Ava Lin

Best Friend!

VICKY FANG

CANDLEWICK PRESS

This is a work of fiction. Names, characters, places, and incidents are either products of the author's imagination or, if real, are used fictitiously.

Copyright © 2024 by Vicky Fang

All rights reserved. No part of this book may be reproduced, transmitted, or stored in an information retrieval system in any form or by any means, graphic, electronic, or mechanical, including photocopying, taping, and recording, without prior written permission from the publisher.

First edition 2024

Library of Congress Catalog Card Number 2023943723
ISBN 978-1-5362-2969-1 (hardcover)
ISBN 978-1-5362-3726-9 (paperback)

24 25 26 27 28 29 LBM 10 9 8 7 6 5 4 3 2 1

Printed in Melrose Park, IL, USA

This book was typeset in Sweater School.
The illustrations were created digitally.

Candlewick Press
99 Dover Street
Somerville, Massachusetts 02144

www.candlewick.com

To Taso and Leo

CHAPTER 1

My name is Ava Lin. I'm six and a half years old. I'm really good at drawing and finding treasure and balancing pasta on my nose.

There is a Very Exciting Thing happening in my life right now. Tomorrow is my first day of first grade!

First grade means I get to play on the big playground and I get to take out two books from the school library every week. Plus, I got a new backpack and a new pencil box and a new lunch box! Actually, I got two lunch boxes.

3

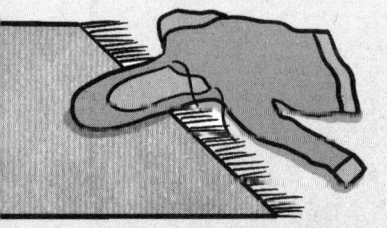

Getting ready for first grade is so much fun. I even almost got a pet!

So... now that I'm in first grade, I'm a big girl, right?

That's right!

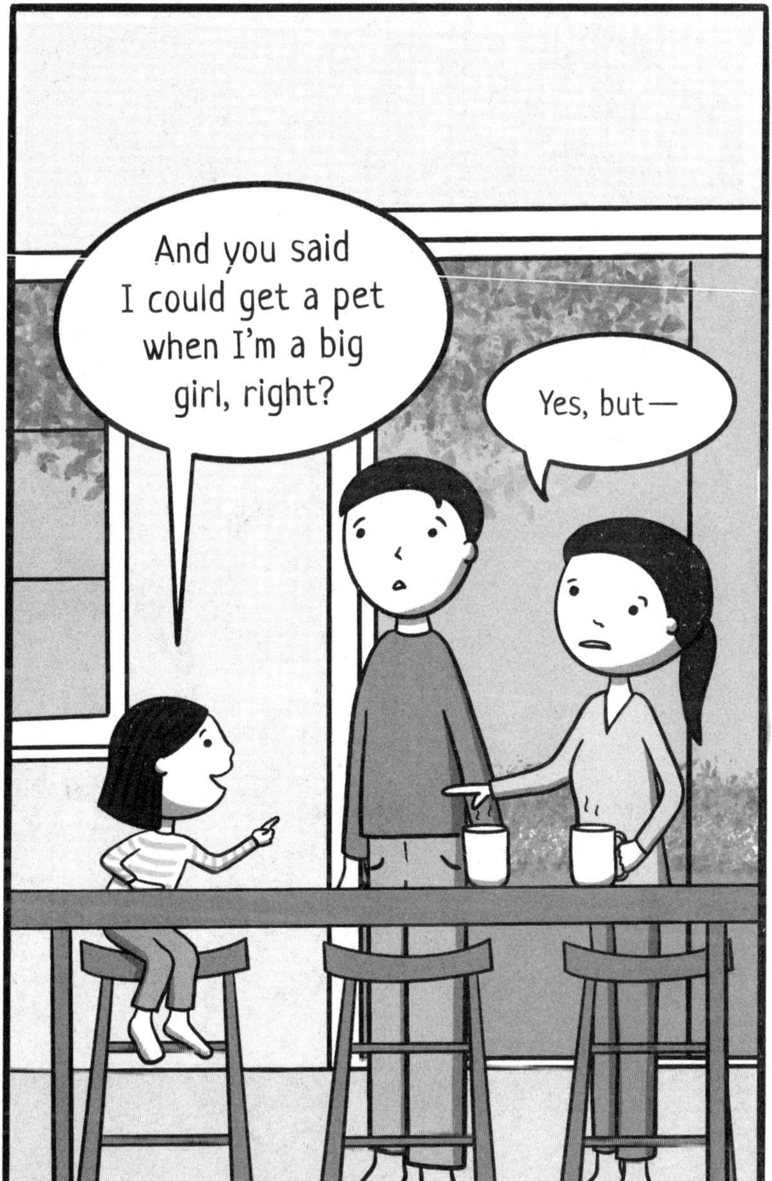
And you said I could get a pet when I'm a big girl, right?
Yes, but—

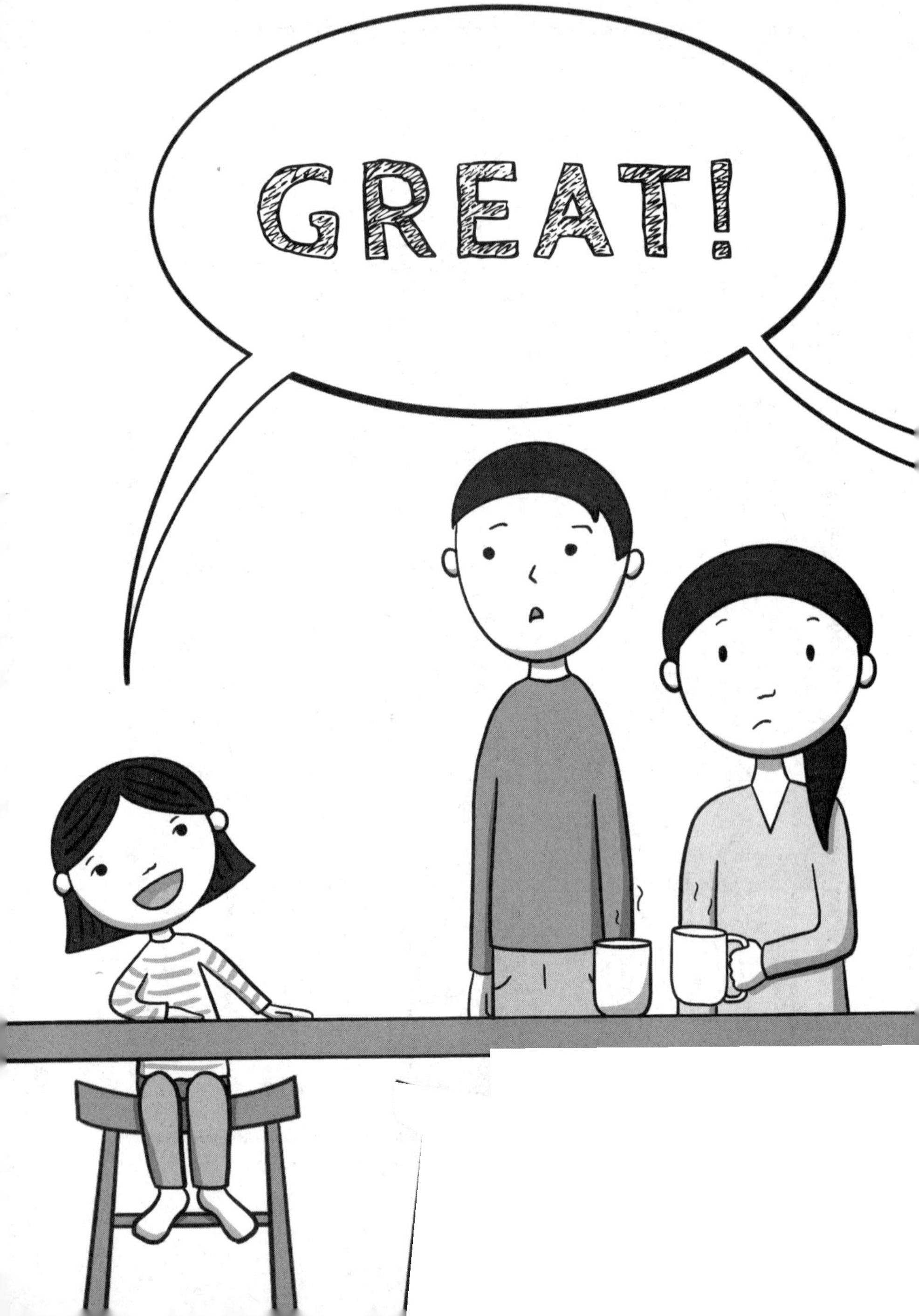
GREAT!

I want a narwhal! Or a dumbo octopus. Or a dragon if they're real, but if not, then a platypus!

Turns out I can't get a pet until I'm ten. I can't wait. I already have a wish list of my top 117 pets!

PEt Wish List
1. Narwhal
2. dumBo octopus
3. dragon
4. pLatypus
5. Meerkat
6. banana slug
7. Hippopotomus

I would tell you the whole list, but I have something more important to tell you right now.

I need to make a

BEST FRIEND.

My cousin Nikki is in fifth grade, but she met her best friend in first grade. So I have to find one THIS YEAR. Don't get me wrong: I made lots of friends in kindergarten. But I didn't make a BEST FRIEND. A best friend plays with you all the time. A best friend always picks you first when making teams. A best friend makes sure you get a good spot on the swings at recess. Having a best friend would be amazing! If I had a best friend, there are so many things I would do with them:

Hunt for treasure

Find the Loch Ness Monster

Draw pictures

Build a robot

Eat ice cream

Discover a new animal species

I really, really, really want a best friend.

That's why I am standing by the door with my coat on and my shoes on and my lucky cat erasers in my pockets. We are going to dinner tonight, and Nikki is going to be there. I need to ask her how to find a best friend.

CHAPTER 2

Dinner is at a big Chinese restaurant with my cousins. They're not really my cousins. Our parents are all just friends, but we call them our aunties and uncles. All the kids are older than me, except for Baby Jojo. Jojo cries ALL THE TIME. I can make her laugh, though.

How to make Baby Jojo laugh:

1. Surprise!

2. Funny face

ha ha ha!

3. Super weirdo wacky dance

The best part about this restaurant is that they have bubble tea. I love bubble tea! Mom almost never lets me have it, but she always does when we come here.

yummy milk tea →   ← sweet tapioca balls

When we get to the restaurant, I run to the kids' table and grab a seat next to Nikki. That's the good news. The bad news is that Justin sits on my other side. Justin is the WORST. He is always making fun of me and playing mean tricks. I'll just ignore him and talk to Nikki.

Nikki has a notebook with her. She is drawing in it.

I wish I had a notebook.

I really want to draw. But I really, really need to ask her about best friends.

How do you make a best friend?

I don't know. You just do.

You just *do*? What does that mean? Justin pokes me.

I say it a bit more loudly than I meant to. But he KNOWS my name isn't Evelyn. I see my mom look at me from the grown-ups' table. Her mouth is smiling, but she doesn't look happy.

I look at Nikki to ask her more questions, but she's still busy drawing in her notebook. So maybe I'll draw, too.

I unfold my paper napkin.

Can I borrow a pencil?

Sure.

Nikki slides the colored pencils between us. They are so pretty.

I draw a dumbo octopus. Number two on my pet wish list, but my number-one favorite thing to draw. When I'm done, it looks so good!

I was so busy drawing, I didn't even notice that my bubble tea came.

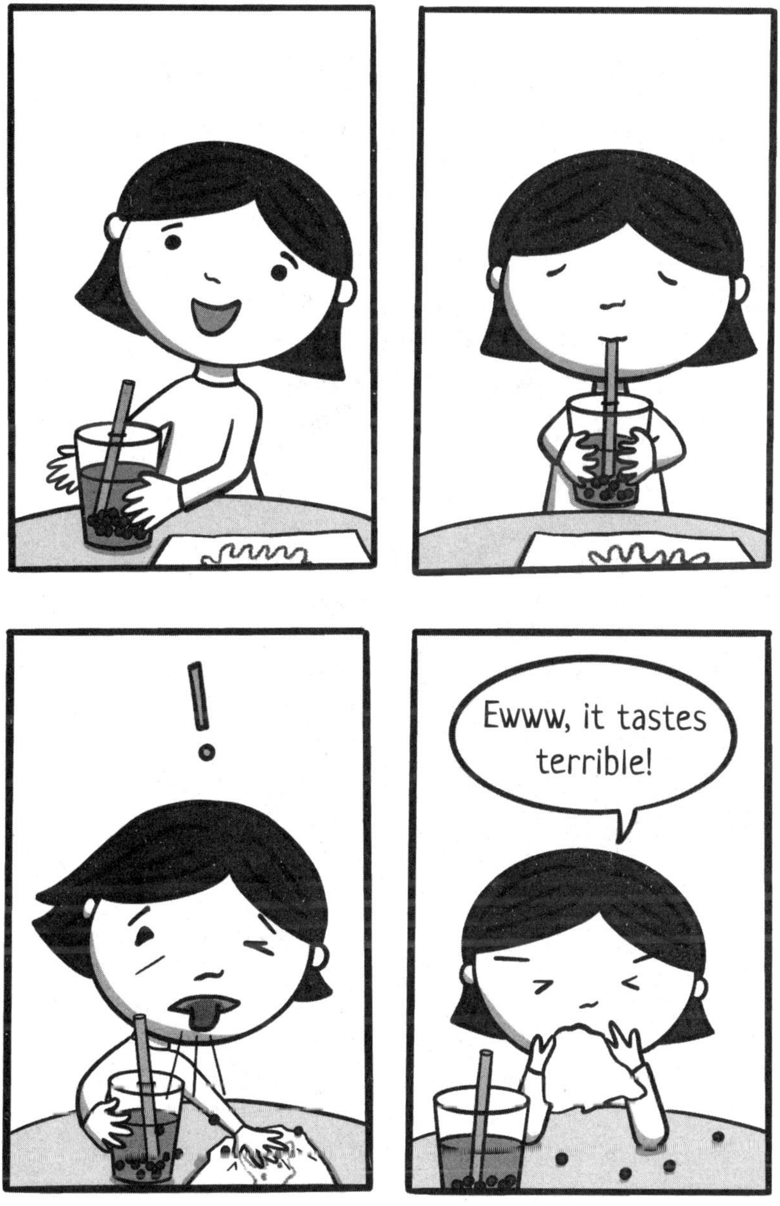
!
Ewww, it tastes terrible!

Ack! I pull the napkin out of my mouth. Some of it is stuck to my tongue. I scrape it off.

My octopus drawing is ruined! And my plate is covered in snarfed-up tea! And my tea is disgusting!

Then I notice that Justin is laughing so hard, bubble tea is coming out of his nose.

What did he do to my bubble tea?

CHAPTER 3

I yell.

WHAT DID YOU DO TO MY BUBBLE TEA?

Justin can't talk. He is shaking with giggles. He just points at the soy sauce bottle. And then I understand.

You put soy sauce in my bubble tea?!

That's why it's so salty and gross!
I am mad. I am SO MAD.
Then I feel tears on my cheeks. Oh, no. I don't want to cry right now! I am MAD, not a sad crybaby!

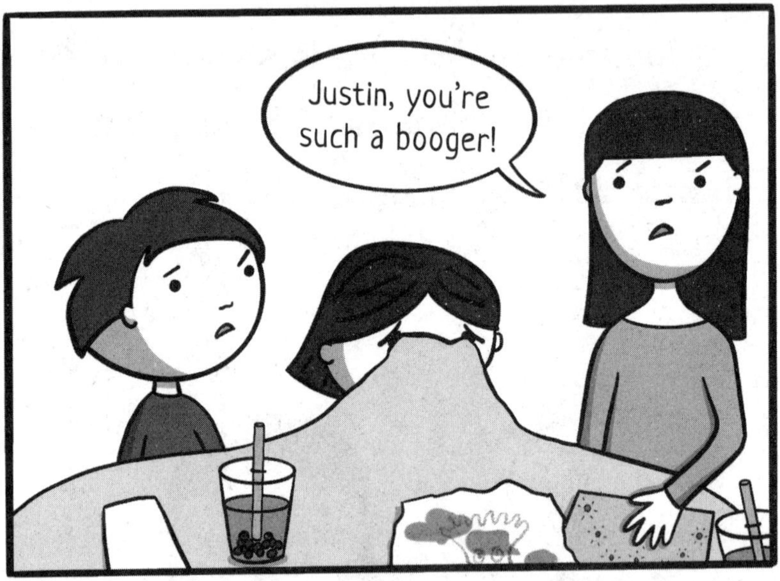
Justin, you're such a booger!

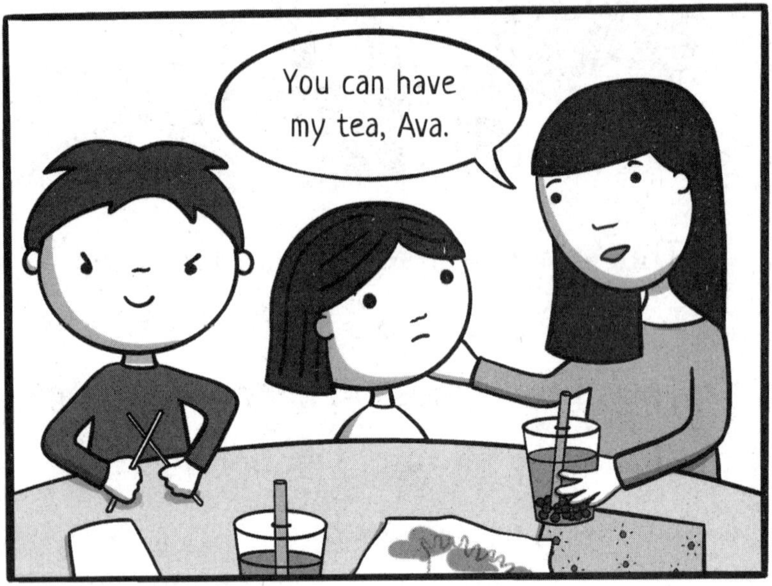
You can have my tea, Ava.

Nikki is so amazing. I nod and take the tea from her.

And that's when I see it.

Nikki's notebook is closed now. And on the cover is her name. She's drawn the letters: *N-i-k-k-i*. But that's not the most amazing part. Over the *i*'s, she's put little hearts instead of dots! They are WONDERFUL. And then all around her name are beautiful jewels stuck on in a starburst pattern. Shiny, sparkly little jewels.

A waiter brings a plate with lots of my favorite foods. There's a little blue fire in the middle, like a mini volcano. Justin is shouting, "Pupu platter!" and laughing his head off. Usually, I laugh, too.

blue → fire

yummy food ↙

But not tonight. I'm not thinking about Justin. I'm not thinking about how funny the words *pupu platter* are. I'm not even thinking about the food or the bubble tea or Baby Jojo crying in the background. I'm too busy staring at Nikki's amazing notebook.

I need a notebook like THAT.

CHAPTER 4

The next morning, I wake up extra early. It's the first day of first grade!

← new backpack

my pencil case

one of my lunch boxes

lucky dress, with FOUR pockets

My school is called Spaulding Elementary. The school mascot is an owl. I love owls! They're number sixty-two on my wish list. Did you know owls can turn their heads all the way around to face the back? I've tried, but I can't get mine all the way around. At least not yet.

Ava, please face forward.

My dad drops me off at my classroom. I'm in Classroom 3 with

Ms. Montgomery. She has curly brown hair and big white sneakers. She is wearing an owl shirt. I like her already.

Welcome! Find the chair with your name on it, and have a seat.

WELCOM
FIRST GI

I look around the classroom. There are ten small tables. Each table has two chairs facing the front of the room. I find my chair at one of the tables in the front row. My name is written on it:

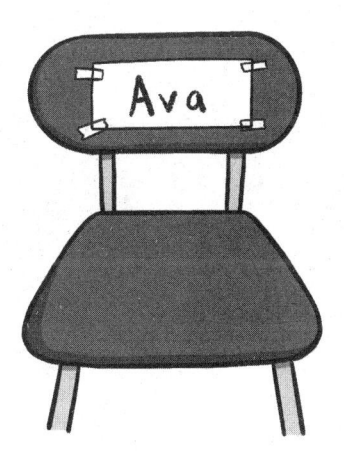

It looks so boring. I wish *Ava* had an *i* in it so I could make a little heart dot like Nikki.

A girl sits down next to me.

"Hi, I'm Kushi."

"Hi, I'm Ava."

Kushi is wearing pink from head to toe. She has a fox on her backpack. I love foxes! Number twenty-two on my wish list!

Maybe Kushi will be my best friend!

After everyone has found their seats, Ms. Montgomery starts talking. There are twenty kids in our class. She calls us Spaulding Owls. I think that's funny. It sounds like "bulding owls."

Ms. Montgomery is talking about the calendar. Then she talks about activities. Then she talks about something called "bucket filling." She says we get prizes if we fill up our buckets by doing nice things. I love prizes!

Suddenly, I see something shiny stuck to the leg of my desk. What is it?

It's a tiny jewel! It's just like the ones on Nikki's notebook! This one is a sparkly dark blue. I pull it off. I stick it in my pocket. What an amazing find!

← sparkly blue jewel!

I miss the rest of what Ms. Montgomery says because I can't stop thinking about that jewel. It is the most beautiful thing I have ever had in my pocket. I love it.

Which makes what happens next even worse.

CHAPTER 5

At lunchtime, I sit with Kushi, a boy named Tristan, and another girl, named Chloe.

Kushi is eating some crispy, crunchy thingies. They look delicious. She must see me looking at them, because she offers me one.

Want one?

I panic. I'm pretty sure it's rude to accept food from somebody. At restaurants, the grown-ups always argue and say no.

"No, no, no, you have it!"

"No, no, you!"

So I politely say no.

"No, no, no. You have it!"

Kushi shrugs and eats the delicious-looking crispy, crunchy thingy.

I panic again.

I should offer her something now!

But I've already eaten my sandwich and all of my crackers and my applesauce.

Why didn't I eat more slowly?

Why didn't my mom pack more lunch?

And then I have an idea.

> I bet Kushi would really like to see the jewel in my pocket.

> And it would be so nice to offer it to her!

> So *best friend—like*! And then she'll politely say no and I'll put it back in my pocket.

> This is a good plan.

I pull the jewel out of my pocket. I hold my hand out toward Kushi. Her eyes widen.

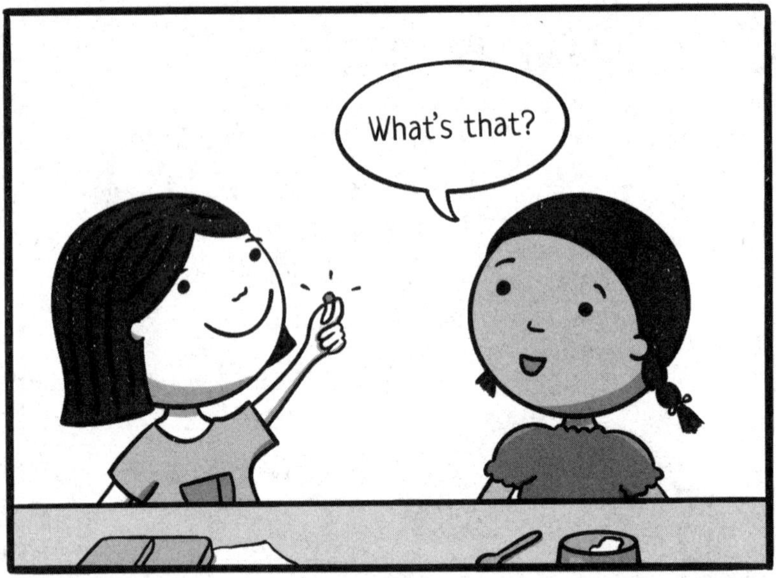
What's that?

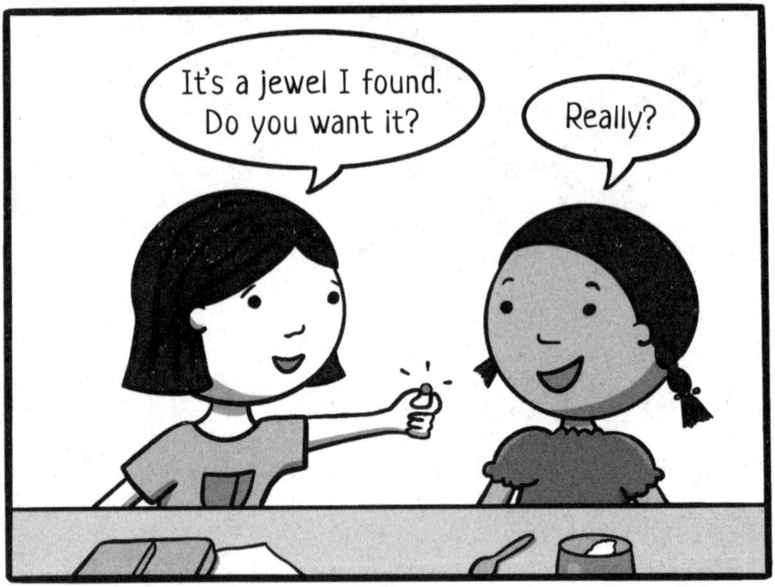
It's a jewel I found.
Do you want it?
Really?

I'm not sure what to say. I think about what the grown-ups would do.

Kushi takes the beautiful sparkly jewel and puts it in HER pocket!

That wasn't what was supposed to happen! Doesn't Kushi know she is supposed to say no?

I don't think Kushi will be my best friend anymore.

CHAPTER 6

When I get home from school, my mom asks how my day was. I can't stop thinking about the blue jewel that is now in Kushi's pocket instead of mine.

Terrible!

I say it louder than I mean to.

My mom tries to ask me questions, but I don't want to talk about it. I'm pretty grumpy for the rest of the day.

I miss my blue jewel so much. I just really, really want it back. I suddenly want to talk to my parents. But I already told them I DIDN'T want to talk to them. I can't go ask them to talk to me now.

I start crying. I think if my mom and dad hear me crying, they'll come talk to me.

I cry for probably one hundred hours before my dad comes to talk to me. I'm so relieved when he finally comes.

I tell him what happened. He rubs his hand on my head.

"Oh, sweetie. I think it was just a misunderstanding. It was nice of you to offer Kushi the jewel, but you should only offer something if you mean it."

And if somebody offers you something that you want, you can take it.
But you don't do that with your friends at the restaurant!

That's different. We're grown-ups. And you're probably right. We're being silly.

I sniffle. I do feel less upset. But I still don't have the jewel. It's gone FOREVER.

Tomorrow will be better—I promise.

I don't see how. What could possibly make up for that lost jewel?

CHAPTER 7

The next day at school, three AMAZING things happen.

After my dad drops me off, I find the most wonderful teensy, tiny snail shell! It was just sitting on the ground under a plant right next to where we line up for school. Can you believe it? It's not every day you find something that special. It feels even more special because it's from nature. Way more special than that blue jewel!

Second, at lunchtime, Kushi offers me a crispy, crunchy thingy again. I say yes. It is delicious! She says they're made out of puffy rice. She says I can have another one tomorrow. Maybe she will be my best friend after all!

But the third thing is the best thing.

Ms. Montgomery gives us our very own notebooks!

I can't believe it. It's not exactly like Nikki's, but I love it. The cover is sort of shiny red. It has little speckles on it, like the whole cover is a jewel! It's the most beautiful notebook I have ever seen. I can't wait to put my name on it.

I write my name in big letters: *A-v-a*.
I tape the tiny snail shell to the cover.

That looks amazing!

For the rest of the day, I collect all kinds of treasures. You won't believe what I find! I put everything in the pockets of my hoodie.

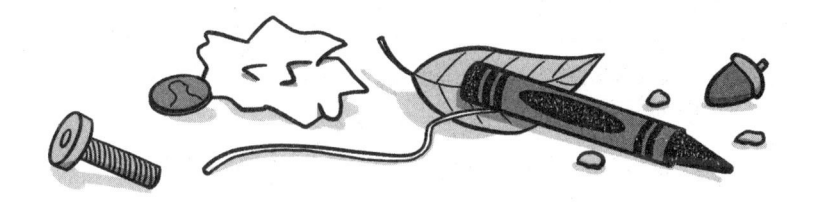

Treasure!

When I get home, my mom takes my backpack and hoodie from me so I can go play. I forget all about the treasures. I am too busy making a dragonfly (number ninety-nine on my pet wish list) out of pipe cleaners. Did you know dragonflies were around in dinosaur times? How cool is that?

Then I hear my mom scream.

CHAPTER 8

"AVA!"

She sounds really mad. I've never heard her so mad. Except for the time I cut up one of her shirts to make a pirate scarf.

She is in the laundry room. I see her holding my hoodie. It's covered with weird black marks.

"Yes, Mom?"

"Ava, WHAT was in your pockets?"

"Treasures."

She points at the laundry basket.
All of the laundry is covered with

black marks. She points inside the dryer. The dryer is covered with the same black marks.

I forgot about the crayon. Ugh! I feel really bad about the black marks. But that crayon was a great find! And it's pretty interesting what happened to it in the dryer. I wonder what it might look like if I put a whole bunch of different color crayons in the laundry.

Oh, right. I thought it was one of those questions I don't need to answer, but I guess it is the kind I do need to answer. I speak very quietly.

I nod. I wonder where I should put crayons from now on, but I think it's better not to ask that out loud.

My mom breathes in a big breath. That's what she does when she's trying to calm down.

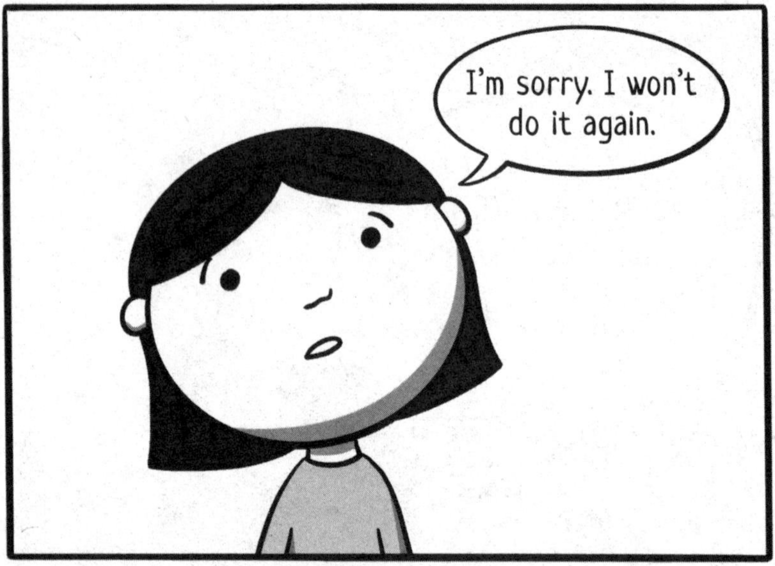
I'm sorry. I won't do it again.

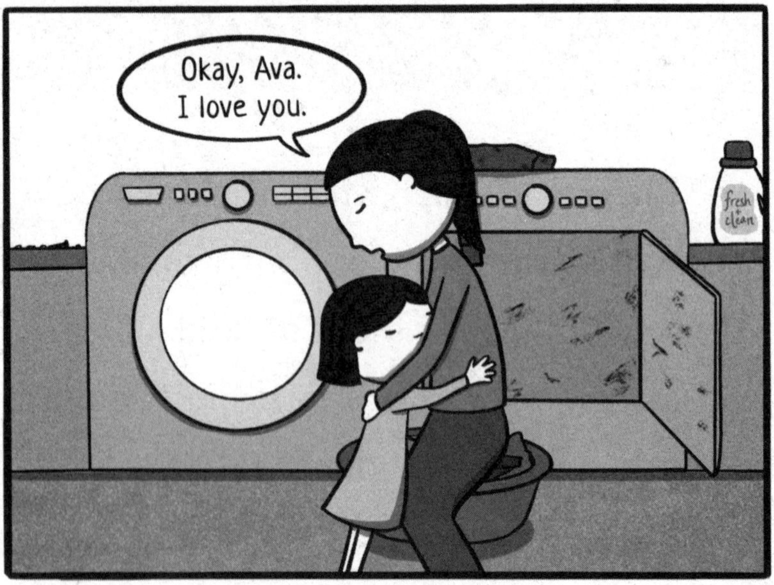
Okay, Ava. I love you.
fresh + clean

I really am sorry. I'm glad she still loves me. When she turns back to the dryer, I spy the rest of my treasures on the counter. I quietly grab the lucky penny and tiptoe out of the room.

CHAPTER 9

The next morning, I notice that my mom has picked out clothes for me with no pockets.

But... I need pockets!

No pockets today.

I can't believe it. I ask her when I will get pockets back. She tells me not today. It is so unfair!

> I can't go to school without pockets!

> Ava. There are no pockets today.

She must be really mad about the dryer. At first, I think I will refuse to go to school. But then I remember that Kushi is going to give me a crispy, crunchy thingy. So I nod and smile and put on my clothes. I can tell my mom is pleased.

When I get to school, I find out we're doing . . .

AN ART PROJECT!

There is construction paper and glue and tons of tiny pebbles in little bins. Each bin is a different color, and there is every color in the rainbow!

I love pebbles!

I am so excited to work on my project. I decide to make an underwater scene.

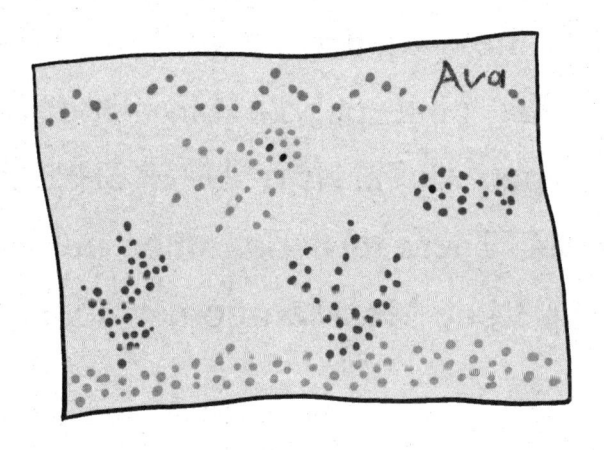

I use lots of blue pebbles for the water. I use orange pebbles for the fish. I make coral out of pink pebbles. And seaweed out of green pebbles.

It looks so pretty!

And then I find something amazing.

a silver pebble

I'm not kidding! I find it mixed into the pink pebble bin. One tiny silver pebble. This is a SUPER SPECIAL pebble. There are no other pebbles like it. I see Ms. Montgomery coming my way.

My heart is bumping. What if she sees the special pebble and takes it away? What if I'm not supposed to have the special pebble?

What should I do?

I want to stick the pebble in my pocket, but I don't have any pockets!

Ms. Montgomery is almost at my table.
I need a pocket! I need this pebble!

So I stick it in my ear.

CHAPTER 10

The pebble is stuck. After Ms. Montgomery passes my table, I try to get it out of my ear. The harder I try to get it, the farther in it goes! I start to panic. What if I can never get it out?

Ms. Montgomery comes to ask me what is wrong, but I have no words. I just keep trying to get the pebble out of my ear. When she finally looks into my ear and sees the pebble, she gasps.

Did you put a rock in your ear?!

Yes!

It was silver!

Ms. Montgomery makes me tilt my head and jiggle it around, but the rock still won't come out.

So Ms. Montgomery takes me to the principal's office, and I have to sit here until my mom comes to pick me up. The principal's office is nice. There's a big squishy green chair and pictures of dogs on the walls. I'm wondering if I should move dogs up from number seventy-two on my list when my mom arrives.

    I can tell my mom is not pleased.

    Her face is all squished up like something is pinching her nose too hard. She looks into my ear for a long time. She keeps pushing air out of her nose like a bull.

Is there
something wrong
with your nose?

No, Ava. There
is nothing wrong
with my nose.

She puts me in the car, and we drive to the doctor's office. The doctor's office! Now I feel nervous.

Am I going to get a shot?

She tells me to just please be quiet. We go into the waiting room, and she tells me to sit down. I sit down across from a TV. It's playing my favorite movie, *Sparkle Chicken*. It's about a chicken that wants to be a famous movie star but nobody sees how sparkly she is. I can only hear out of one ear, but I've seen the movie so many times, I pretty much have it memorized.

Sparkle Chicken

When my mom comes to sit with me, her nose looks less squeezy. But she doesn't laugh when Sparkle Chicken gets dizzy from spinning in the talent show. That's my favorite part. I laugh lots.

I don't get to see Sparkle Chicken win the talent show, because it's our turn to see the doctor. We go into the office and I sit on the crinkly paper thingy. Dr. Longfellow comes and talks to me and my mom about the pebble in my ear.

She looks in my ear. She has a light thingy stuck on her head. It is cool. I wish I had a light thingy to stick on my head. Then she uses some long pinchy thingy and pulls the rock right out of my ear.

My mom finally smiles. And stops breathing like a bull.

So, no more rocks in your ear, okay, Ava?

Or anything else, Ava. Seriously.

Okay! Can I keep the rock?

My mom snorts. Dr. Longfellow holds out the rock in the pinchy thingy. I take the rock. But where should I put it? My mom tries to take it, but I know she will just lose it. I stick it in my sock instead.

Dr. Longfellow laughs again. She gives me a sticker. As we leave the office, I look at the sticker.

ALL BETTER!

I look at the explanation point on the sticker. I love explanation points! They look so cool.

> Why is there an explanation point here?

> Exclamation point. An exclamation point adds excitement to the words.

Ex*cla*mation point. Ugh, that sticks in my throat. I like *explanation point* better. I think about explanation points for the whole car ride home. I know exactly what I want to do with an explanation point.

CHAPTER 11

That night, I can't sleep. So much to think about. I'm thinking about explanation points, and I'm thinking about treasure, but I'm also thinking about best friends.

I think about how Nikki and her best friend do everything together. Kushi and I kind of do everything together, but really, the whole class does everything together.

What can Kushi and I do together that is special?

CHAPTER 12

The next morning, I notice my clothes have pockets again. That's good. I really need pockets today. Today is officially my fourth day of first grade. Well, maybe it's only my third and a half day, since I had to leave early yesterday. But today, I have . . .

A PLAN.

My pockets are full of treasures. My snack bag is full of snacks. My head is full of ideas.

After morning greeting and science lab (I love science lab!), it's finally lunchtime. Kushi hands me a crispy, crunchy thingy. This time, I have a snack to share, too! I open my packet of teriyaki seaweed. I see Kushi's eyes get wide. But just as I'm about to give some to her, Ms. Montgomery comes rushing over.

Oh, no, no, no! Have you been sharing food!? No sharing food!

It turns out we're not actually allowed to share food at school because of allergies. This is terrible! I didn't even get to eat the crispy, crunchy thingy that Kushi gave me! And if lunchtime went so badly . . . what if the second part of my plan fails, too?

After we finish our lunch, I squeeze the lucky penny in my pocket.

lucky penny →

Hey,
Kushi . . .

Do you want
to decorate our
notebooks together
during recess?
Yes!

It's a success! We spend the rest of recess working on our notebooks. I share my treasures with her, but I keep the most special ones.

I tape each of my treasures onto the cover of my notebook:

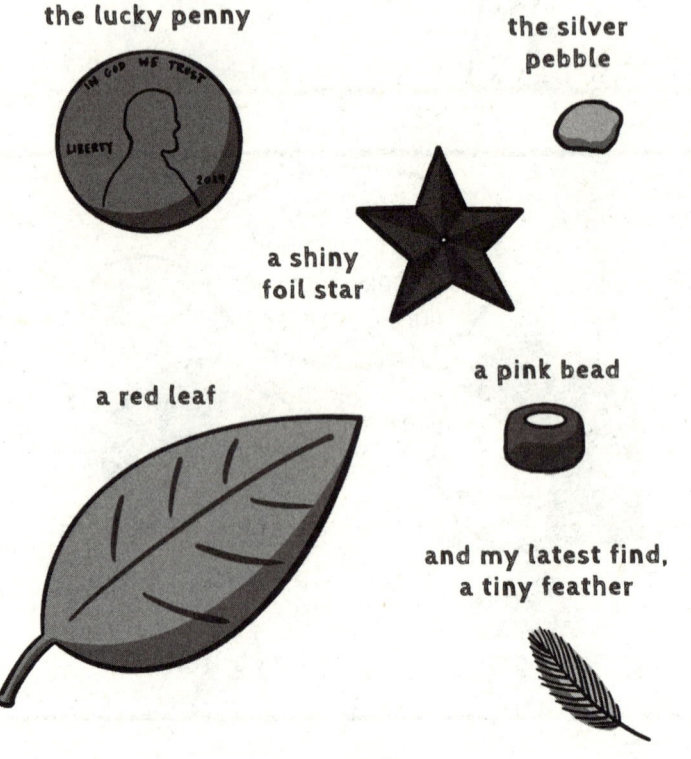

the lucky penny

the silver pebble

a shiny foil star

a red leaf

a pink bead

and my latest find, a tiny feather

When we're done, we have the most beautiful notebooks. Really. I cannot stop looking at my notebook. It is perfect. The best part is the heart dot!

I'm so glad I got to do something special with Kushi.

I don't know if Kushi is my best friend yet or not. I'll have to ask my cousin Nikki the next time I see her. But I do know one thing for sure:

First grade is amazing. With one hundred explanation points!